First published in 2017 by Nosy Crow Ltd
The Crow's Nest, 10a Lant Street
London SE1 1QR
www.nosycrow.com

ISBN 978 0 85763 645 4 (HB)
ISBN 978 0 85763 644 7 (PB)

Nosy Crow and associated logos are trademarks and/or registered trademarks of Nosy Crow Ltd.

Text © Jeanne Willis 2017
Illustrations © Jarvis 2017
The right of Jeanne Willis to be identified as the author of this work and of
Jarvis to be identified as the illustrator of this work has been asserted.

A CIP catalogue record for this book is available from the British Library.

Printed in China by Imago
Papers used by Nosy Crow are made from wood grown in sustainable forests.

1 3 5 7 9 8 6 4 2 (HB)
1 3 5 7 9 8 6 4 2 (PB)

For Blake – love from Aunty Jeannie x

For Jenna – Jarvis

I'm In CHARGE!

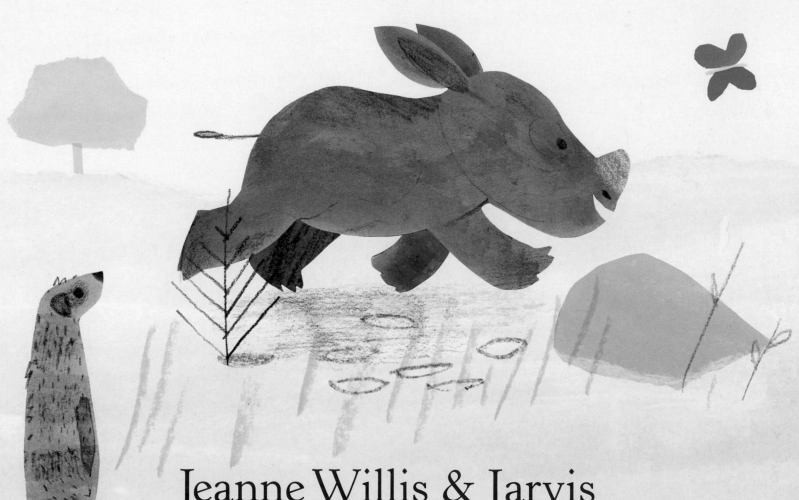

Jeanne Willis & Jarvis

nosy crow

There was once a little rhino
who was really rather large
and from the day that he was born
he bellowed, "I'm in charge!"

So when his darling daddy

tried to tell him what to do,

he cavorted and he snorted,

"Daddy, I'm in charge – not you!"

And when his muddy mummy
told him when to go to bed,
he shouted, "No, I will not go!"

"I'm in charge!" he said.

He did exactly as he pleased
and **threw** his weight about.

When Warthog tried to cross his path,

he **tossed** him with his snout.

He **scattered** all the meerkats
and he **startled** poor Giraffe.

He **squashed** Baboon's banana when
he would not give him half.

Now, Elephant was larger, but young Rhino didn't care.
It wasn't hard to charge her, if she could not see him there.

He sneaked up to the waterhole and gave his tail a thrash,
then **barged** her in the bottom. "I'm in charge!" he said

. . . ker-splash!

And so he was
until the day
the mango tree
grew fruit,
which Rhino just
refused to share.
He did not
give a hoot.

He put his little foot down, and if anyone came near . . .

he shouted, "Shoo! No fruit for you!
Hey, I'm in charge round here!"

No one dared to challenge him,

then Pygmy Mouse came by.

She was tiny but so hungry

that she thought she'd have a try.

"No, you are **not** in charge," she said.

"The fruit is **ours** to eat!"

But Rhino would not listen,

and he **stamped** his feisty feet.

"I'm not listening – la la la! I'm in charge . . . Agreed?"
he yelled and so he never heard the sound of a stampede.

"Stand back!" said Mouse to Rhino.

"You'll be sorry if you don't."

But Rhino took no notice.

"Rhino rules!" he said. "I won't!"

"This fruit is mine – all mine!"

he said. "I'm not afraid of you.

I am scared of nothing!

No one tells me what to do!"

Pygmy Mouse then backed away
as Rhino **scoffed** the fruit.
"I'm glad you know who's boss,"
he grinned, the **greedy** little brute.

Mouse waved her tiny paws about.
"Look out! A herd!" she cried.
But Rhino would not hear a word,
and did not step aside.

But then to Rhino's horror
as he'd almost had his fill . . .

. . . a **hundred** beefy wildebeest

. . . came **charging** down the hill.

Too fast to stop, they thundered past.
They made a **dreadful** sound!
They **stomped** on all the mangos . . .

. . . as the tree fell to the ground.

"Those wildebeest have **wrecked** my feast!"
cried Rhino. "And my tree!"

Then Mouse said, "Rhino, who's in charge?"

And Rhino said . . .

. . ."Not me!"